"Be a lion. You are the king or queen of your jungle!"

Bea Lion: Breaking Free

Copyright ©2021 Becky Cummings

authorbcummings@gmail.com

ISBN: 978-1-951597-19-1 (hardcover)
ISBN: 978-1-951597-20-7 (paperback)
ISBN: 978-1-951597-21-4 (ebook)

Library of Congress Control Number: 2021910125

Illustrations by Margherita Grasso
Editing by Laura Boffa and Sam Pendleton
Cover Design by Praise Saflor

First printing edition 2021.

FREE
KIDS
PRESS

BEA LiON
Breaking Free

Written by Becky Cummings

Illustrated by Margherita Grasso

FREE
KiDS
PRESS

Bea the lion was born at the zoo.
Her cage was all she knew.

Each day was the same.
Bea always had meals delivered by Frank the zookeeper, water to play in after her mud bath, and bars to protect her. While she appreciated being clean, comfortable and calm, she felt something was missing.

"Mom, I want to leave this cage and explore the world," said Bea.
"Don't be silly! This is where you belong," replied Mom. "Out there, a
coconut could fall on your head. An alligator could eat you for lunch.
In here, we have everything we need."

Mom feared the worst, but Bea did not. She felt brave. Bea gazed up at the birds flying overhead.

Watching them flap freely in the breeze made her belly tickle with excitement. "There is so much more. I must go and see," she whispered. "I will break free, but how?"

She could bite Frank the
zookeeper and leap out.
But she was too nice.

She could dig her way out.
But that was too tiring.

Bea paced back and forth in her cage, thinking. Suddenly, a big splash of bird poop hit her on the head. It was Rosie Spoonbill.

"Dirty bird. Keep your poop to yourself!" Bea shouted.

Now she would need to lick herself for hours. That's when Bea got a crazy idea. What if she didn't clean herself? What if she got really dirty? So yucky that Frank would have to take her out of her cage for a bath.

Bea would need help. When her mom and dad were in a deep sleep, she let out her jungle roar. Mom had told her it was only for emergencies. This felt like one. Bea's roar attracted a lot of attention. Spoonbills, pigeons and even a pelican circled overhead.

Bea spotted Rosie Spoonbill and shouted,
"Hey, you pooped on me earlier!"

Rosie turned even pinker.
"It was an accident, pardon me.
I'm so embarrassed," she said.

"Well, I need you to do it again.
And bring your friends, too,"
Bea begged.

Rosie's eyes lit up, "Have you lost your mind Bea?"
Bea got quiet, "Can you keep a secret?
I'm breaking out of here and I need your help."
"I'm not sure how pooping on your head is going to help," giggled Rosie

"Just trust me. I must get extremely dirty," Bea said.
"Bea, this is big. Why do you want to leave?" asked Rosie.
Bea's eyes got watery.
"I just want to be free, like you, my friend."

"Then I will do what it takes to help you.
Tomorrow, we birds will have a pooping party."

The next morning, Bea went for a swim.

Then she rolled in the dirt.

The sun baked the dirt into her fur.
She looked more like a bear than a lion.

"Bea, you are acting strange today. Are you okay?" asked Mom.
"Just feeling a little hot, so I thought I'd do what the hippos do," Bea
replied. Mom shook her head. "Bea, you're the cleanest lion I know.
What is really going on?"

"I'm sorry, Mom. I didn't want to disappoint you.
The truth is I plan to leave the zoo," said Bea.
"But you're supposed to stay with us," Mom said sadly.
"I know it's not common to leave. But I choose to be different," replied Bea.

"Okay, my sweet Bea. I want you to be happy and follow your heart." Mom smiled.

"I will never forget you, Mom. I will come back one day for you and Dad. I'd hug you, but..."

Just then, Bea heard the squawks in the distance.
"Mom, take cover!"
The squawks got louder and louder.

The birds assumed position. Rosie led the countdown. "One, two, three, fire!" It rained poop.

Milky white goo covered Bea. She was a hot mess. She was ready for Frank.

Minutes felt like hours. Bea sat still, waiting.
She kept reminding herself, I can do hard things.

Finally, Frank made his dinner rounds.
"What on Earth, Bea! I can't even see your fur!
I will have to take you for a bath."

Frank slipped a collar around her neck and led her out of her cage. Bea turned and looked at her mom. She let out a gentle roar and blinked with love.

Frank led Bea into another fenced-in area behind the cage. Bea looked around for an escape.

Rosie was sitting on the fence above a gate. She flapped her wings gently. Bea understood.

It was time. Bea grabbed the leash from Frank's hand and tugged. He dropped it in shock.

"Bea, what are you doing?"

With the leash in her mouth,
she dashed for the door. Using all her
might, she pushed it open. Bea was free.

Bea sprinted as fast as she could.
Frank was shouting. An alarm was ringing.
She kept running.

Rosie swooped down.
"Follow me," she called.
Bea followed the pink bird.
She ran through a maze of cars.
Her paws felt hot against the smooth
black ground. She kept going.

"Don't stop!" Rosie squawked. Soon,
Bea was surrounded by tall, thin trees. Her
paws hit something she had never felt before.
Then Bea saw something she had never seen
before. It was the biggest tub of
blue water with no sides.

Rosie landed beside her.
"Welcome to the ocean. You are
safe. Now please go take a bath!"

Bea laughed, "This is beautiful!" She charged for the water and jumped into the waves. She was free at last.
The world would be her playground.

And that's when Billy saw her.

Enjoy Other Books by Becky Cummings:

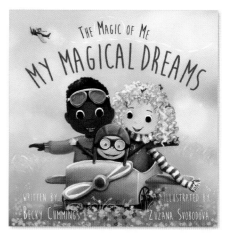

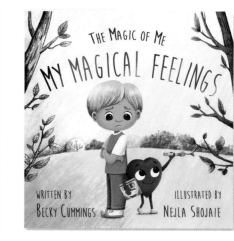

Also Be Sure to Check Out:

The Magic of Me: A Kid's Guide to Creating Happiness
Gobble Gobble Mr. Wobble
Share Share Ms. Hare